That Terrible Halloween Night

by JAMES STEVENSON

GREENWILLOW BOOKS / New York

Library of Congress Cataloging in Publication Data

Stevenson, James (date)   That terrible Halloween night.   Summary: Grandpa tells Louie and Mary Ann of the dreadful Halloween night that turned him into an old man. [1. Halloween–Fiction]   I. Title.   PZ7.S84748Th   [E 179-27775 ISBN 0-688-80281-8   ISBN 0-688-84281-X lib. bdg.

"What day is today, Grandpa?" asked Louie.
"Today?" said Grandpa. "According to the paper, it is
  October 31, and the paper is generally correct."
"Grandpa doesn't know tonight is Halloween," said Louie.
"Oh, boy," said Mary Ann.

"What can we do to scare Grandpa?" said Louie.
"Something not <u>too</u> scary," said Mary Ann. "Grandpa's pretty old."
"I have an idea," said Louie.

They put a mask on Leonard.
"Now go see Grandpa," said Louie.

"GRRR," said Leonard.

"Good dog," said Grandpa, giving him a pat.

"We better try something a little <u>more</u> scary," said Mary Ann.

"Woo-oo!" said Mary Ann.
"I beg your pardon?" said Grandpa.

"<u>Wooo</u>!" said Mary Ann, even louder. "<u>Wooo</u>!"
"Why are you sitting on Louie and wearing those
strange clothes?" said Grandpa.

"To scare you," said Louie.
"It's Halloween."
"Oh, of course," said Grandpa. "I see."
"Were you scared?" asked Mary Ann.

"Yes, indeed," said Grandpa.
"But I don't get very scared anymore—not since that terrible Halloween night."

"<u>What</u> terrible Halloween night?"
"I prefer not to talk about it."
"Please, Grandpa!"

"A long long time ago, when I was about your age,
I put on a moustache and a hat, and ...

I went out on Halloween.

I knocked on doors up and down the block, getting candy.

Then I came to a strange house.

There was a light inside, and I heard some terrible noises.

I didn't know whether or not to go inside ...
Do you think I should have gone inside?"

"I went up the steps.

When I opened the door bats flew out.
I heard awful wailing and screeching, but I went inside.

It was very dark.

At first I couldn't see anything ...

except the yellow eyes."

WHAT YELLOW EYES?

"The big ones at the top of the stairs...
with the huge pointed teeth.

I walked up the stairs ..."

"It was only a giant spider. It ran away giggling.

At the top of the stairs I saw a pumpkin coming toward me.

I ran for the stairs.

Suddenly the stairs gave way.   I fell down and down.

I landed in the cellar.

It was cold and dark and wet and smelly and ..."

"It was hard to walk because the floor was entirely frogs–very slippery.

I kept getting caught in the cobwebs.

Then I heard a horrible voice.

Then I saw an awful creature.

But it was the only door, and I wanted to get out.

I opened the door.   It was the worst mistake I ever made!"

"But when I came out of that house, I was an old man.

And I've been that old <u>ever since!</u>"